Scenes From Family Life

Mark Ravenhill

A Samuel French Acting Edition

SAMUEL FRENCH

FOUNDED 1830

SAMUELFRENCH.COM
SAMUELFRENCH-LONDON.CO.UK

FOR PRODUCTION ENQUIRIES

UNITED STATES AND CANADA
Info@SamuelFrench.com
1-866-598-8449

UNITED KINGDOM AND EUROPE
Plays@SamuelFrench-London.co.uk
020-7255-4302

Each title is subject to availability from Samuel French, depending upon country of performance. Please be aware that *SCENES FROM FAMILY LIFE* may not be licensed by Samuel French in your territory. Professional and amateur producers should contact the nearest Samuel French office or licensing partner to verify availability.

SCENES FROM FAMILY LIFE was first produced by the Kildare Youth Theatre in the Cottesloe Auditorium of the National Theatre as part of the National Theatre London's New Connections Programme in London on July 7, 2008. The performance was directed by Keith Burke and Peter Hussey.

CHARACTERS

All characters are aged 16 – 18

JACK

LISA

STACY

BARRY

A GROUP OF THEIR FRIENDS

THREE SOLDIERS

PARENTS AND BABIES GROUP

MOTHER WITH AN EMPTY PRAM

ENTERTAINER

SETTING

Living room of Jack and Lisa's flat

Scene One

(Living room of **JACK** *and* **LISA**'s *flat.)*

LISA. Feel?

JACK. Yeah.

*(***JACK*** reaches out and touches* **LISA**'s *stomach.)*

LISA. Head and feet and… Tiny but somewhere there's…

JACK. Yeah.

LISA. You thought of names?

JACK. Not yet. You?

LISA. A few but… Don't want to jinx it.

JACK. Too soon.

LISA. Yeah.

JACK. What's it feel like?

LISA. Different.

JACK. Does it send you messages and stuff? Through your body?

LISA. I dunno. Maybe. Yeah.

JACK. You gotta know.

LISA. No.

JACK. What's going on in your head?

LISA. Happiness. You. Me. Baby.

JACK. That all?

LISA. Yeah.

JACK. You sure…?

LISA. I can't tell you every –

JACK. But that's what I want to know.

LISA. It's just not possible. You ready to be a dad?

JACK. I am totally, totally ready.

LISA. My mum she says we're too young but I say Jack's got
    a job, I got a job, we got the flat, it's time. I love you.
JACK. And I love you.

> *(They kiss.)*

Together forever. You feel trapped?
LISA. No. Love it. Love you.
JACK. Am I boring?
LISA. Normal.
JACK. I'll get the tea.

> *(Exit* JACK. *Woosh, flash,* LISA *vanishes into thin
> air. Re-enter* JACK.*)*

Lisa do you want white or the…? Lees? Lees? Lisa?

> *(pause)*

Lisa?

> *(pause)*

Lisa!

> *(pause)*

Lisa?

> *(He hunts around the room.)*

I'm gonna find you and when I find you I'm gonna…
Lisa?

> *(He goes and checks in the bedroom.)*

> *(off)* Lisa!

> *(He enters from the bedroom. She reappears – a
> rematerialisation.)*

Oh my god. Oh my oh oh –
LISA. What? What?
JACK. I… There was nothing there. It was frightening.
    There was like this gap where a person should be and I
    was calling out but there was nothing there. And then
    you were there.
LISA. Stop messing around.

JACK. I'm not I – Oh Lees. You think I'm going mad? Maybe…

LISA. Forget it. Trick of the light. Kiss me.

JACK. Listen I…can't.

LISA. You're scared of me.

JACK. No just I –

LISA. You are. You're scared of me.

JACK. Of course if you can just –

LISA. I'm solid – I'm real – you see – you see – touch me – touch me – what do you feel?

JACK. Yeah solid, real yeah.

LISA. So I'm here. Nothing happened. You're very tired. You're very stressed. Nobody's running away. Nobody's fading. I'm here with you. We're gonna have the baby together. We're gonna be together – forever. Yeah?

JACK. Yeah. Yeah. Yeah.

LISA. Daddy.

JACK. Mummy.

LISA. You feeling alright now?

JACK. Yeah.

> *(Whooshing sounds. Flashing lights. She's vanished.)*

Oh no oh no oh no oh – hello hello hello – oh no please! Are you there? Are you – oh oh oh oh. Oh please don't do this oh please oh – I don't want to be on my own. I don't like being on my own. Oh oh oh.

> *(Flashing and whooshing. Blackout. Full light.*
> **LISA** *is back.)*

LISA. Can I do the curry now?

JACK. You did it again. You vanished. Faded away and then –

LISA. You're mad.

JACK. Stop doing it.

LISA. This is completely mad.

JACK. I want you to stop doing that. I don't like it.

LISA. I'm not doing anything. I'm living with a freak.

JACK. There's a place up there or down there or in there or…somewhere and you are going there.

LISA. I have enough of this. I've wanted this baby ever since I was thirteen and now you, you – I'm going out.

JACK. Where?

LISA. I don't know. Shops. Cinema. Mates. Anywhere.

JACK. But what if you vanish –? In front of your mates?

LISA. Not gonna happen. Good night.

JACK. Stay here.

LISA. Why?

JACK. It'll be safer.

LISA. You're making me frightened.

JACK. With the current circumstances.

LISA. There are no…

JACK. I'll look after you. Stay. Stay. Stay in the house. How we gonna look after baby if you don't stay in the house?

LISA. How can we if you keep –?

JACK. It's not me it's you who's vanishing.

LISA. See. See. We're incompatible.

JACK. No no I do love you Lees I do, I just – something's going on – I don't understand but there is something but I – oh – but I do want the baby so…

LISA. Alright but – listen – you gotta cut out the funny stuff. I want normal. That's important.

JACK. I'll try to cut out the –

LISA. Normal. Yeah – I just can't handle. There's a world out there of people and they're all odd. They seem odd. They have like freak outs on buses and stuff. Talk to themselves. Punch strangers. I can't handle that. You're normal. That's why I picked you.

JACK. Course.

LISA. I gotta have a totally normal baby father.

JACK. I'm the one. Maybe I'm…tonight means so much I'm just…didn't think I was nervous but maybe I'm…

LISA. Come here.

JACK. Yeah.

> (*Whooshing, flashing etc.* JACK *rapidly gets out his mobile phone. Starts video recording.* LISA *vanishes.*)

Come on come on.

> (*Wooshing flashing etc,* LISA *reappears.*)

You did it again.

LISA. No I never I was just –

JACK. You did. Look.

> (JACK *rewinds the images, indicates to* LISA *to have a look on the phone.*)

LISA. This is stupid I'm not gonna just –

> (*Reluctantly, she looks.*)

…Oh my god. Thin air and then I…that's so frightening. Hold me. Oh babe.

JACK. (*holds her*) I know, I know.

LISA. Am I solid now? I feel solid.

JACK. You are. You're solid now.

LISA. What we gonna do? If I'm the kind of person who just vanishes – I don't wanna be the kind of person who just vanishes. I never heard of that…people who just… oh.

JACK. Me neither.

LISA. I want to be here forever.

> (*doorbell*)

JACK. I'll do it.

> (JACK *answers it. Enter* BARRY *and* STACY, *who is eight months pregnant.*)

BARRY. Will you tell her, will you tell her –?

STACY. Just watch him.

BARRY. Will you two tell her –? Will you tell her – she's got this idea, she's got this really stupid idea –

STACY. It's not –

BARRY. She says that I'm vanishing. She says –

STACY. He has.

BARRY. I haven't.

STACY. You have. You fade in front of my eyes – you go to nothing.

BARRY. Will one of you, both of you, tell her that she is mad? Hormones.

STACY. I'm not –

BARRY. People don't just vanish. I try but I – it's the baby playing with her hormones she doesn't – When women are pregnant they get these…your head gets muddled up. You cry and then you're happy and then I vanish.

JACK. Barry mate –

BARRY. Yeah? *(to* **STACY***)* Listen to this –

JACK. Barry mate it's true. People vanish. Lisa's doing the same. Today I've seen –

BARRY. Jesus.

JACK. Three times. People vanish. I never thought 'til today. But I've seen it. You can just…lose people. They fade to nothing. Empty.

> *(beat)*

BARRY. *(to* **STACY***)* You set him up to this.

STACY. I didn't do nothing.

BARRY. Lisa?

LISA. It's true. I'm not a solid person. I'm a person who just…goes and comes back again.

BARRY. You're all mad. What you been doing? Well, I'm not going to vanish. Why am I gonna vanish? I'm not gonna vanish. Not gonna vanish when I got a kid on the way.

LISA. Show him the clip.

JACK. Look at this.

(He shows **BARRY** *and* **STACY** *the phone clip.)*

LISA. See? I go to nothing.

BARRY. ...Oh my god... Is that what I...?

STACY. Just the same. Same as you.

BARRY. Oh no. But I want to be in this world. All the time. I don't want to miss stuff. I'm not choosing to go – do you choose...?

LISA. I didn't know anything. I thought it was all normal 'til –

BARRY. I wouldn't choose... I want to be with you.

STACY. What if you vanish when the baby's born? Can't have you vanishing once the baby's born. That's not a role model. I want a two parent family. I gotta have – That's what it's about isn't it? A mum and a dad. I'm not gonna be a sad cow pushing a kid round by myself. That's not what I –

BARRY. Course, course.

STACY. Feels bad when you're gone.

JACK. *(to* **LISA***)* Yeah – feels really terrible.

LISA. Stop watching that clip.

JACK. I was just –

LISA. You are – you're just watching it over and over.

JACK. Well...

LISA. Feels really weird you doing that.

JACK. Just want to see if maybe there's some...

LISA. Don't. Delete it.

JACK. No.

LISA. I don't like it. It scares me. Delete it.

JACK. It might – it's evidence.

LISA. I don't care. It's doing my head in. Give it me. Give it me.

JACK. No.

LISA. I want it. Don't want you looking at that over and over. Fading disappearing nothing. Fading disappearing nothing. Fading...

BARRY. She's right.

JACK. Alright alright. I'll look, look…

> (**JACK** *goes to delete but whooshing, flashing etc.*
> **LISA** *and* **BARRY** *disappear.*)

Oh. No.

STACY. Barry! Barry! This is doing my head in.

JACK. How many times it's happened to you?

STACY. Four, five times since breakfast. This is my sixth.

JACK. Does it get any easier?

STACY. No. Still hurts. In your gut. Your heart. Whatever. Miss him.

JACK. Yeah – me too.

STACY. I couldn't ever get used to a vanishing person.

JACK. Maybe we'll have to.

STACY. I can't.

JACK. But if this is, like, the way it's gonna be.

STACY. Then I just can't handle the way it's gonna be.

JACK. You'll have the kid.

STACY. If it's a stayer. Maybe the kid'll be a vanisher too.

JACK. 'Spose.

STACY. If the dad's a vanisher then maybe the kid's a vanisher too.

JACK. You still want it?

STACY. Yeah only…

JACK. You'll cope whatever won't you? Vanisher or stayer?

STACY. I suppose I don't – this is so new. Vanishers. Stayers. I didn't know there was a difference when I woke up this morning.

JACK. Terrible innit?

STACY. Yeah. Terrible.

JACK. This could be rest of our lives.

STACY. No.

> (**BARRY** *and* **LISA** *reappear.*)

Back again.

BARRY. Did we…?

JACK. You faded away – you dematerialised. You went somewhere –

LISA. Oh god. What do you think we are – aliens?

JACK. I don't know.

LISA. I don't want to be an alien or a ghost. Hold me.

JACK. You go out with someone, you live with someone

STACY. You get pregnant with someone –

JACK. And then they turn out to be a vanishing person.

LISA. Hold me.

JACK. I'm frightened.

LISA. We're not aliens or ghosts. Hold me. I think we'd know if we were aliens or ghosts wouldn't we Barry?

BARRY. I think so.

LISA. And we'd let you know so don't – Hold me. Hold me. Hold me. I'm totally frightened. I'm totally freaked. So don't just look at me like that staring. Come and hold me.

JACK. I'm sorry.

(He holds her.)

LISA. Please don't say those terrible things about us.

JACK. Sorry.

LISA. Give me a kiss.

JACK. …I can't. Not yet. Sorry babe.

LISA. Oh. I just can't take this. It's doing my head in. I got a kid on the way. But you won't even kiss me. It's too…

*(Whooshing, flashing etc – **LISA** vanishes.)*

JACK. Oh my god. This is too much. This is gonna drive me mad. I can feel my mind turning. I'm losing it. Losing it. Agggghhhhh!

STACY. Come on. Sssssh. Sssssss. She'll be back.

JACK. I suppose.

STACY. They always come back. Barry's always come back. Barry's here. Look Barry's here.

BARRY. That's right. I'm here for you mate, yeah? She's bound to come back. Everyone always comes back.

JACK. So far. What's she up to – up there?

STACY. Don't know.

JACK. She could be up to anything right now.

STACY. Well I suppose.

JACK. Aliens. Aliens experiment on you don't they? Oh yeah. I've seen it in documentaries. They abduct you, abduct you up to their spaceship and experiment on you. They could be putting an alien baby inside her. Taking out my baby and…

STACY. I don't think Barry's been experimented on have you?

BARRY. No. I'd feel it wouldn't I? I feel like myself. I feel normal. It's you lot act different when I come back. I don't think there's experiments.

JACK. You don't know that. They'd wipe you.

(pause)

She's been gone a bit long hasn't she?

STACY. Not that long.

JACK. Was Barry ever this long?

STACY. Well I'm not sure…

JACK. It was just a few seconds before. Only ever a few…

STACY. Yeah.

JACK. What if she doesn't come back?

STACY. She will.

JACK. We don't know that. She could have vanished forever.

(long pause)

Look she's not coming, she's not coming back…she oh my god she's not coming back. I've lost her. I loved her and now I lost her.

STACY. Give it a bit more time.

JACK. I think we should do something.

BARRY. Give it time.

JACK. It's alright for you – you're one of them – You're an alien or a ghost or whatever but me and Stace we're normal –

BARRY. I'm normal!

JACK. Oh no – you go to the secret places, the secret place of the vanished, you've seen the secret place, you don't come back from there normal. *(to the sky)* Give her back, send her back, send Lisa back to us...come on!

(**BARRY** *vanishes.*)

STACY. Barry! Barry! Oh god.

JACK. I'm sorry Stace.

STACY. This is stressing me so much. I'm only two weeks off my due date I shouldn't be stressing like this. This can't go on forever. Can't live days like this. What we gonna do?

JACK. I dunno – maybe scientists or doctors maybe they'll sort it.

STACY. You reckon?

JACK. Or the government.

STACY. Yeah right.

JACK. Or, or, or maybe it's like a – those poltergeist –

STACY. Stupid.

JACK. They'll be something – it'll be okay. Something'll work out.

STACY. I hope so. Not back though are they?

JACK. No.

STACY. You really having a baby?

JACK. Yeah. want this. Until I got a kid, I'm a kid.

STACY. Same for me... They've not come back.

JACK. They will.

STACY. Yeah?

JACK. They will and then we're gonna stop this.

STACY. How we gonna...?

JACK. Maybe if we just hold to them. Hold onto them really tight and don't let them go.

STACY. Forever?

JACK. Well…

STACY. You can't just hold onto someone forever.

JACK. We could try. Just 'til the vanishing's over.

STACY. Oh.

JACK. What?

STACY. Something. Baby moving.

JACK. Can I listen?

STACY. Yeah?

JACK. I'd like to. *(He listens.)* Oh yeah.

STACY. Really – oooo. Better not be – oooo –

JACK. What?

STACY. Contractions. No. I'm alright. Baz has gotta be here if –

JACK. Yeah. I'll look after you if –

STACY. Yeah?

JACK. Make sure you're up the hospital and that you know if you start –

STACY. But you're not the dad.

JACK. No. I know that.

STACY. It's not the same.

JACK. All I'm saying –

STACY. It has to be the dad. It has to be Baz.

JACK. But if he's not here –

STACY. He's got to be here. I need him here. I want him here.

JACK. Yeah but all I'm saying if he's vanished forever.

STACY. He hasn't.

JACK. They're not –

STACY. Nobody vanishes forever. *(clutches stomach)* Ooooo.

JACK. 'Nother listen?

STACY. It's not a game.

JACK. Please.

STACY. No.

> *(Doorbell rings. Exit* **JACK***, reenter with a group of friends [names and genders can be changed here to suit your group]:* **KAREN, HOLLY, TONY, MATT, MARIE, JAMES** *– all talking at the same time.)*

KAREN. Listen, listen. Something's happening. Something's going on. We've all been vanishing. All of us. We were all round Holly's house and then like Matt vanished first didn't you –

MATT. That's right.

KAREN. But then Matt came back again. But then it was Marie, James, me.

TONY. And me.

KAREN. One at a time until it was like: who's next? Who's going to go next? Stick together guys 'cos we don't know who's going to go next.

HOLLY. We are seriously frightened.

> *(Enter* **RYAN***, running after them.)*

RYAN. It's happening all over the world.

KAREN. Yeah?

RYAN. Been on the news. Everywhere there's people fading away to nothing. They've got footage from China, America, India – everything. Nobody knows the figures. One in ten. That's what they're saying. One in ten people has already gone but the numbers keep going up – with every minute there's more and more.

JACK. They could be nobody.

KAREN. Don't.

JACK. By the end of today there.

MARIE. Let's pray.

MATT. What's that gonna do?

MARIE. We gotta do something. *(kneels)* Oh Father who created this world and made everything in it and is now taking away everything in it have pity on us poor children. Spare us spare us spare us.

*(**MARIE** continues to mutter a prayer under.)*

STACY. I feel so close.

JACK. Yeah?

STACY. It might happen. What if it happens? I don't want to have my baby like this.

JACK. Ssssssh. Whatever it is – we'll cope.

STACY. I want Barry. Barry! Barry! Barry!

JACK. Stace – no – you musn't upset yourself – you'll bring it on – Stace!

STACY. Barry!

*(**MARIE** vanishes.)*

HOLLY. Marie. When's it gonna end?

MEGAPHONE. *(off)* This is the authorities. Stay in your homes. I repeat: stay in your homes.

JACK. Oh my god.

MEGAPHONE. Anyone leaving their home without authorisation will be shot. We are investigating the vanishings but you must stay in your homes.

*(Enter **TWO SOLDIERS**.)*

SOLDIER 1. Whose house is this?

JACK. Mine.

SOLDIER 1. The military has taken control. This country is now under military control.

JACK. Oh my god.

SOLDIER 1. *(raising gun)* Keep calm.

SOLDIER 2. No harm will come to you if you do exactly as the army say. We are requisitioning a number of houses in which to herd the civilian population – and your house has been selected as a suitable centre for civilians. Do you understand?

JACK. I think so.

SOLDIER 1. *(who's been listening on an earpiece)* They're ready to bring in the other civilians.

SOLDIER 2. Good – let's get them in here.

SOLDIER 1. *(calls off)* In here.

SOLDIER 2. Your home is to be the base for the parents and babies group. This way, this way.

> *(***SOLDIER 3*** marches in a huge range of different parents and babies: single parents and couples, papooses front and back, and buggies, prams – some with twins, triplets. The noise of crying babies fills the air.)*

SOLDIER 3. That's it – make room, make room – if you squeeze in – you gotta make room.

SOLDIER 1. *(pointing gun)* Calm and orderly – that's it.

SOLDIER 2. Room for everyone.

> *(Finally everyone is in – but it's a very tight squeeze.)*

SOLDIER 1. *(with megaphone)* Everyone sit down. We have to keep order. We have to keep control. Each parent must take responsibility for controlling their baby. No baby is to crawl or in any way move from their buggy or papoose. It is vital that we keep calm. Let's organise entertainment. Can anyone juggle, dance or offer any skills that might amuse the babies?

> *(A **MAN** or **WOMAN** comes forward.)*

WO/MAN. Me.

SOLDIER 1. Please entertain the children.

> *(The **WO/MAN** begins to break-dance or juggle or play the ukelele – or anything else that might entertain a large crowd of parents and babies – but after a while wooshing, flashing etc. **LISA** appears. The crowd gasps. Entertainment stops.)*

JACK. Lees?

LISA. I got to speak to Jack. Where's Jack?

JACK. I'm here. Are you alright Lees?

LISA. No. I'm hurting. Oh!

(She collapses.)

JACK. Come on love. It's alright.

LISA. Who are all these people?

JACK. You did another vanishing Lees.

LISA. Yeah?

JACK. Lots of people are vanishing. It's happening all over.

LISA. Ugh. Hurt.

JACK. We were gonna have a quiet night in weren't we?

LISA. It's all gone wrong.

JACK. It'll go back to normal – everything always goes back to normal.

LISA. It won't. It's not gonna because…

JACK. You'll see everything'll get sorted. We'll be a family.

LISA. I want to come back to you – I do.

JACK. You're back now babe.

LISA. I'm trying to break through but I can't. I can't stay this time. The pull's too strong.

JACK. Stay Lees. Forever. I need you here.

LISA. I can't. I have to go. I loved this world. I loved you. That's all I wanted. But I'm lost to this world. I'm lost to home and shopping and baby and work and you. All that's gone now. I have to be in the other world – I have to –

JACK. Lees – no – don't do that – see all the babies here Lees? See 'em?

LISA. Yeah. Pulling back to the other world.

*(Woosh, flash. **LISA** vanishes. Panic in the crowd.)*

MARIE. Oh my god that was so horrible – that was like the most horrible thing I have seen in my life ever.

RYAN. Do you think she'll come back?

JACK. Maybe gone forever.

SOLDIER 2. Order, order – we must have order.

JACK. Lisa? Lisa?! Come back come back.

SOLDIER 2. Steady there.

JACK. I love you. I want a baby.

SOLDIER 2. Stop or I shoot – you're spreading panic.

JACK. But I have to have her. She's everything I need –

SOLDIER 2. *(raising gun)* I have permission to shoot trouble makers.

JACK. Shoot me then go on. What's the point? That's my future just vanished. Better shoot me now. They've all got babies. You've all got babies. That's what I want. Give me a baby. Give me a baby. I want Lisa back so we can have our baby and fill up the world again. Don't you look at me like I'm nutter. Just 'cos you got your babies. Could be me. Should be me with a baby.

> *(Woosh, flash – a third of the people in the room vanish. Pandemonium. Babies howling, parents offering toys and bottles, cooing.)*

SOLDIER 1. Everybody calm!

KAREN. I don't want to go. I don't want to go. Please don't take me.

RYAN. It's the end of the world. The end of everything.

HOLLY. This is like the most horrible thing that's happened to me ever.

> *(A young **MOTHER** steps forward from the crowd and talks directly to **JACK**.)*

MOTHER. My baby. The pram's empty. Look – an empty pram. My baby was three weeks old. But already her eyes followed me around the room. Baby once. Now – empty pram.

JACK. It'll all come right.

MOTHER. How you know that?

JACK. I don't…

MOTHER. There's two languages. You got kids or you haven't got kids. And if you haven't got a kid you don't speak the language. It's a love, it's a something, a –

JACK. Yeah – but –

MOTHER. Sorry. You're just a kid – you don't understand.

JACK. Maybe. But I'll understand – yeah. Very soon I'll understand when Lisa –

MOTHER. You'll never get your chance. You missed your chance. This is it. This is the world ending. No more people.

JACK. No.

MOTHER. You say your goodbyes. Now my kid's gone all I want is I go too – listen to all them babies crying. Soon be gone now.

(Woosh, flash – total darkness.)

Here we go. We're fading away. All fading away.

(The room empties of people. Silence.)

JACK. Hello? Hello? Anyone there? Anyone there at all?

(JACK uses a lighter to create a little bit of light.)

Is there anyone left? Or am I the only person left in the world? No please don't do that. I don't want to be the only person left in the world. That's horrible. See I won't know what to do if it's just me 'cos I need people to talk to and to do things with. I don't exist if there's no one else. I'm nobody without other people. What are they all doing in the other world? Is there another world? Come on – take me there – I don't want to be like this forever.

(He finds a candle and lights it.)

STACY. Jack – is that you? Have they all gone?

JACK. I don't know.

STACY. Hello? Hello? They've all gone.

JACK. It's just you and me.

STACY. In the world – do you think it's just you and me in the world?

JACK. Could be… I don't know.

STACY. What are we going to do Jack?

JACK. I don't know Stace.

STACY. Jack –

JACK. Yeah?

STACY. I'm contracting.

JACK. What do you mean?

STACY. The baby. My contractions.

JACK. Are you sure?

STACY. Yeah – oh – oh – yeah – I'm sure.

JACK. How long have we got?

STACY. Few hours.

JACK. Maybe they'll come back. Maybe all the doctors and nurses and midwives and everything'll be back in time.

STACY. Maybe.

JACK. Yeah – we just gotta be brave, we just gotta stick it out and –

STACY. Oh oh oh oh oh. It's the stress – brought it on. Oh.

JACK. What we gonna do?

STACY. I don't – oh oh oh oh oh. What if they don't come back?

JACK. They will. They've got to.

STACY. How do you know that?

JACK. I just…believe.

STACY. But it could be you and me and that's it. We could be the human race.

JACK. No no.

STACY. Oh. Bigger contractions.

JACK. Can't you control it?

STACY. No – I can't. I wish I could. But I can't.

JACK. *(to sky)* Please – come back. All of you – come back.

STACY. Jack – face it. They're not coming back. They're never coming back.

JACK. You're scaring me.

STACY. This is the world. You and me. And I'm just about to have – oh – once my water breaks that's it you're gonna have to – you're doctor and midwife and –

JACK. Why me?

STACY. Because there's no one else.

JACK. Right.

STACY. So get ready.

JACK. Yes. Okay, okay. I can do this. I can.

>(**JACK** *cuddles* **STACY**.)

You…breathe and calm and when you're breathing and calm and –

STACY. They'll be mess and pain and everything.

JACK. It's okay. I know.

STACY. You'll have so much to do.

JACK. Both of us.

STACY. Hot water and towels – kitchen paper and and and –

JACK. When we get to that bit. Breathe.

STACY. Yeah.

JACK. Stace. Do you think this was how it was meant to be?

STACY. No I don't. Do you?

JACK. I don't…maybe.

STACY. No – this is not supposed to be. This is not normal. This is…

JACK. The last thing in the world?

STACY. Yeah.

JACK. We're all alone now. Just you and me. Listen to that. Nothing. Babies, traffic. Nothing. I reckon there's no-one. Anywhere. Just you and me.

STACY. Not for much longer.

JACK. No?

STACY. New one on the way. Are you ready?

JACK. I don't know.

STACY. You got to be Jack. You got no choice.

JACK. Yeah. Okay. I'm ready.

Scene Two

(The living room. Six months later. **JACK** *and a baby in a pram.)*

JACK. *(to baby)* And once upon a time there was a brand new world. And the world had no people. Until – pop – there were two people. And they were called Jack and Stacy.

And after a year there were three people in the world 'cos along came a baby. And they called that baby Kelly. You're lovely aren't you Kelly? Yes you are. Your mum's out there somewhere and your mum'll be back soon. And we'll be back together. Family.

(Enter **STACY**, *with a rucksack on.)*

How do you get on?

STACY. Yeah. Not bad. How's baby?

JACK. Baby's good. Took her feed. Nice sleep.

(She opens the rucksack for his inspection of contents.)

More beans?

STACY. Yeah. Sorry. But – look.

(She holds up a packet of nappies.)

JACK. Brilliant. At last.

STACY. Yeah.

*(**STACY** takes out a tin of rice pudding and a tin opener and opens it.)*

JACK. You gonna eat that cold?

STACY. I been hunting all day.

JACK. You get attacked by them escaped lions again?

STACY. No, it's the dogs though. They gone feral. Started hunting in packs. There's a load of them live up the multi-storey car park. You have to watch yourself.

JACK. Still no sign of any humans?

STACY. No.

JACK. I told you.

STACY. Got to keep looking.

JACK. Six months – if there was anyone else we'd have found them by now.

STACY. I suppose.

JACK. Come on Stace there can't be –

STACY. Don't you want people? Don't you want the world?

JACK. I don't know.

STACY. This can't be just – why would it just be us?

JACK. Luck. Fate. I don't know.

STACY. A thousand – a thousand thousand – miles – there's someone else.

JACK. Just you and me and…baby. Stace – don't you think we should give her a name?

STACY. No.

JACK. I mean six months – 'baby' – it might stunt her development, something.

STACY. I know only…

JACK. How long you gonna wait?

STACY. I want to choose it with Baz.

JACK. He's not coming back.

STACY. Don't say that. They're all coming back.

JACK. Yeah… You got blood.

STACY. It's nothing.

JACK. Show me.

(**STACY** *shows his hand.*)

STACY. There was a cat and a load of kittens sat on the nappies. We had a fight.

JACK. See. Told you. Animals are still breeding.

STACY. S'pose.

JACK. She must have met a tom. We gotta look after that.

STACY. It's nothing.

JACK. I'll bandage it.

> (JACK *exits,* STACY *eats rice pudding,* JACK *re-enters with bandage and TCP, etc.)*

JACK. Here we go.

> (JACK *dresses the wound, bandages it while:.)*

They were noisy – humans – weren't they?

STACY. Those elephants down the road make noise.

JACK. Just a few of them. They're lonely. But billions of human beings. That was terrible. It's good that they went.

STACY. Don't you miss Lisa?

JACK. Sometimes.

STACY. I thought you were having a kid.

JACK. Yeah well she's gone now.

STACY. For the moment.

JACK. Six months.

STACY. But if you're having a kid –

JACK. After six months, you move on.

STACY. Move on? There's nobody to… The world's empty.

JACK. Stace – I get lonely in my bed.

STACY. Can't help that.

JACK. Sleep with me Stace.

STACY. No.

JACK. We don't have to do nothing – just share the bed.

STACY. It'll lead to stuff.

JACK. It won't. Last two humans – at least we could share the bed.

STACY. Forget it. It's not gonna happen. Ugh! She needs her nappy changing.

JACK. I'll do it. *(to baby)* Come on Kelly we're going to –

STACY. What did you call her?

JACK. Nothing.

STACY. You called her something. Kelly.

JACK. Just 'til she gets a real name. It's not good for her.

STACY. Oh no, oh no – That is not Kelly right? That is baby. And I'm not having you doing anything different? Understand? Understand? Give me baby.

JACK. I'm gonna –

STACY. Give me – now.

> (**STACY** *and baby exit.* **JACK** *opens a box of cornflakes from the rucksack, starts eating with his hands. Woosh, flash.* **BARRY** *appears.*)

BARRY. Stace? Stace?

JACK. Baz? No.

BARRY. Stace.

JACK. Baz she's –

BARRY. Stace.

> (*Woosh, flash,* **BARRY** *disappears,* **STACY** *re-enters with baby.*)

STACY. Where's them fresh nappies?

JACK. Stace – let's go somewhere. Now.

STACY. What do you mean?

JACK. The whole world's empty. We could live anywhere. Buckingham Palace. Yeah – let's move. Find somewhere else.

STACY. We're fine here. She's used to it.

JACK. No – we got to move now. I'll get some things.

STACY. Don't be mad.

JACK. Make a head start before it gets dark.

STACY. I'm not going anywhere.

JACK. But it's dangerous here. It's not safe here please Stace.

STACY. You go.

JACK. Please Stace you don't understand –

STACY. Go.

JACK. By myself?

STACY. I'm not stupid Jack. I know what you're up to.

JACK. Don't know what you mean.

STACY. Playing families.

JACK. No.

STACY. Well you're not dad see?

JACK. I know but –

STACY. So keep away from her. She's my baby. Me. Baz.

JACK. Alright – you look after by yourself from now on. I'll hunt for my own food.

STACY. You do that.

JACK. I will.

STACY. My baby. You keep off her Jack. Piss off – piss off you – piss off and leave me and my baby in peace.

> (**JACK** *reaches into the rucksack and pulls out a breadknife.*)

JACK. Right – I gave you a warning. This is what we're doing. I'm taking charge. We're moving on. Pack a few things and get down here in ten minutes and we move on or I cut you –

STACY. Go on then. Cut me. I don't care.

JACK. I will.

> (**JACK** *grabs her by the wrists.*)

Where do you want cutting first?

STACY. Jack don't.

JACK. This is a perfect world. Not having that ruined. You're not spoiling it for me Stace. You get born – you think the world's your mum your dad your brothers sisters. That's nice. Then you go to school. You got your mates. And that's good. The world's getting better and getting bigger. Then you go holiday – see all these other places. Bigger and bigger. Then you get on the net and you start chatting and you got friends all over the world. You ever used to do that in the old days Stace – before the vanishing – chat to people all over the world?

STACY. Course. Get off.

JACK. And I thought that was great. Chatting all over the world. But then they go – they vanish, they start to fade away and there's just you and me and me and Kelly.

STACY. She's not called –

JACK. She's called Kelly *(waves knife)* alright?

STACY. No, I don't wanna –

> *(*JACK *slices across her cheek.)*

Oooooooo!

JACK. Kelly. I name our child Kelly. Kelly – tonight from this moment on, now and forever more you are christened Kelly. No godparents. But – what can you…? Kelly. Kelly. *(to* STACY, *wielding knife)* Yes? Yes? Yes?

STACY. Yes. Kelly.

JACK. That's it mummy. Say hello Kelly.

STACY. …Hello Kelly.

JACK. Tonight Kelly – mummy and daddy are going to have a lovely meal of all the food that mummy got up the shops then when mummy and daddy are feeling nice and tired they are going to go to a big house somewhere a long way away somewhere like Buckingham Palace with a big double bed –

STACY. No.

JACK. Big double bed and they're going to take their clothes off and they're going to get into the big double bed. And they're hold each other all night. Mummy's been too shy since you were born to sleep with daddy but tonight she's not going to be shy. Tonight she'll get over that and she'll hold daddy. And maybe if the mood's right they'll have sex. Yeah – maybe if it's an extra special night they'll have sex. Yeah. They'll have sex.

STACY. I'm not gonna do that.

JACK. You'll do just what daddy tells you to do or I'll – because this is all for Kelly, this is all. We got to be normal. Normal family. In a normal family – baby's got a name, mummy and daddy love each other, mummy and daddy have sex, mummy and daddy try for another baby.

STACY. No.

JACK. Kelly all on her own. Not good. Not right. So we start working on a little brother or little sister for Kelly. We start working on that tonight.

STACY. It's not gonna happen.

JACK. It's the normal thing.

STACY. Then I'm not going to be normal.

JACK. You are.

(He slices at her cheek.)

STACY. Don't Jack – no. Is there blood?

JACK. A bit.

STACY. I'll go septic and die.

JACK. No.

STACY. Yeah. I'll go septic and die and then what you gonna do?

JACK. I'm here for you. I'm here to look us all. I'm gonna mend this and then you're gonna pack our stuff and we're gonna move on to our new place. Go and pack.

STACY. I'm gonna change baby. Kelly. Don't hurt her. You can hurt me only…

JACK. I'd never do that. She's everything to me.

STACY. Alright as long as…

JACK. I know what's best. I'm dad.

STACY. Yeah.

(STACY exits with Kelly. Woosh, flash. BARRY appears.)

BARRY. Where's Stace…?

JACK. Still…a long way away…hunting.

BARRY. My kid. Want to see my kid.

JACK. Listen Baz. I gotta tell you…

BARRY. Yeah?

JACK. World's gone bad. Streets are full of wild animals. Baz it's really bad here, you don't wanna, the world's such a bad place. Baz…

BARRY. Yeah?

JACK. And… It's been six months. World moves on.

BARRY. Well…yeah.

JACK. There's no one left in the world Baz – 'cept me and Stace and Kelly. Oh yeah. We called the kid Kelly.

BARRY. But I wanted to –

JACK. Sorry mate. I delivered the baby. Pain like you wouldn't believe for hours. Stace screaming in your face. I found the baby – guided it down. First pair of hands to guide it. Cut the cord. Cleaned them up – mother and kid. I chose the name. I like it. See and now…we got a bond. Stacy. She's mine.

BARRY. No.

JACK. And Kelly – we decided it was best, too confusing see. Not gonna tell her about the world before, the vanished people. Decided to tell Kelly I'm her dad. Mummy daddy and baby.

BARRY. You bastard.

JACK. Maybe. But that's the way things are. So the rest of you can stay up there or down there or out there or whatever because we don't want you. You're not wanted here. So you stay right where you –

BARRY. No!

> (BARRY *punches* JACK *in the stomach.* JACK *collapses.* BARRY *kicks him.*)

My kid. My world.

JACK. Don't want you. Stay in your world 'cos this world's better without you. I'm King here.

> (*Wooshing, flashing,* BARRY *vanishes.* JACK *is winded. Gets up.*)

Alright, alright, everything's okay. Over now.

(Enter **STACY** *with a shopping trolley fully loaded with bags etc, wearing a coat.)*

STACY. Did what you said.

JACK. Good girl.

STACY. Think it's best innit? If I do what you say?

JACK. I don't like forcing you.

STACY. Funny way of…

JACK. Only sometimes I just see. What's best. For the family.

STACY. Right.

JACK. You'll like Buckingham Palace.

STACY. I'll do what you say.

JACK. Stace – you gotta love me.

STACY. That an order?

JACK. That should come natural.

STACY. Well – it's not natural.

JACK. Give it time.

STACY. No. Anything you want you'll have to use that [knife].

JACK. If I have to.

STACY. Yeah you have to.

JACK. Princess Kelly's gonna have her own apartments when she's older. Her own wing. Kensington Palace.

STACY. Let her choose.

JACK. She'll need guiding.

STACY. Oh. Like we all do – yeah?

JACK. Wagons roll.

*(***JACK*** puts baby in the pram starts to push it.)*

Come on Kelly. New home. New start.

STACY. Oh I –

*(***STACY*** staggers.)*

JACK. What?

STACY. I – I – I –

(She collapses.)

JACK. Gotta move. Gotta move on. Come on. Gotta get up. Come on.

STACY. Jack – I'm – oh!

> (*Flashing. Brief vision of the hordes of the vanished. Wooshing. Dies down.* **STACY** *has vanished. Just* **JACK** *and the baby left.*)

JACK. Right. Right.

> (*pause*)

> (*to baby*) Just you and me. Which is…this is…

> (*pause*)

Once there was a new world. And there was just me in it. And I was all alone. And I grew up. And then one day this baby – pop. I called her Kelly. I looked after her. I fought off the animals. I hunted. I had meaning. I was a King and there was a Princess.

That's good isn't it? We're the first and one day they'll be – pop pop – from nowhere more babies but until then…

Yeah. You and me. Empty world.

Right. We'll… Sleep here tonight. We'll move on in the morning.

Night Kelly. (*leans into pram, kisses baby*) Night.

And we all slept sound 'cos we were the only two in the world and there was no fighting.

> (**JACK** *lies down to sleep, closes his eyes. Flashing, whooshing.* **JACK** *leaps up.*)

Kelly!

> (*Brief vision of* **STACY** *and* **BARRY** *carrying away the baby. Wooshing, flashing dies down.* **JACK** *is alone.*)

…Empty pram. Empty world.

> (*long pause*)

I was born into this place of the animals and of the shops and the food and the houses.

And I was the only person. The first and the last.

And so I never thought about it. How could I ever think…? If you never knew there were others then…

But sometimes I dreamt, I imagined there were others. Somewhere – others.

Something in this. [pram]

But that was fantasy. Because the world is just me. Now and forever. And on and on and good good good.

Only ever me.

So why the –? [pram]

A thing from long ago.

> *(beats the pram rhythmically)*

Don't need you. Never need you. Don't know what you're for. You're for nothing.

Nothing. Nothing. Nothing.

You are…a dead thing.

> *(kicks over the pram, carries on kicking it)*

You are a totally dead thing.

I am everything.

I am the world.

So I…

Hunt. Eat. Sleep. Move on. This is my world.

And I…

No if there were never others then there's no loneliness.

No lone…lone…lo…lo…

Lugh. Lugh. Lugh. Lee. Negh. Sssssss.

> *(ape like) Ugh ugh ugh.*

> *(He's becoming more animal, his centre of gravity moving down.)*

I ugh oh a oh a ooo m a ugh.

Me.

Me.

Me.

(pattern of movement, almost dancing)

JACK. *(cont.)* Me.

Me.

Me.

And I.

And I.

And I.

(Onto all floors snuffling and whining. A great animal howl. Then the energy drains from him. Finally, curls up.)

(Flashing, whooshing. **SOLDIER 1** *appears, brandishing gun.)*

SOLDIER 1. Hello? Hello?

*(***JACK*** wakes, snarls.)*

What the –? What is this place?

*(***JACK*** growls, squats, ready to attack.)*

Steady. Steady! – I'll shoot.

*(***JACK*** bares his teeth.)*

Animal.

*(***SOLDIER 1*** goes to fire.)*

You had your warning.

*(***JACK*** leaps at **SOLDIER** 1, biting at him and snarling a tustle on the ground. Wooshing, flashing. The room begins to fill up with the vanished. **JACK** retreats. Soon the room is full of the parents and babies, the soldiers, the friends and **BARRY**, **STACY** and **LISA**. Everyone is talking, calling out. **MOTHER** with the empty pram steps forward.)*

MOTHER. My kid. My kid. Where's my kid?

(She disappears into the crowd searching.)

HOLLY. Has it finished? Is it over? Have all those people stopped vanishing?

(**SOLDIER 2** *comes forward listening on his earpiece.*)

SOLDIER 2. *(on megaphone)* Attention. I have received instructions that it is over. The emergency is now over. The vanished have returned. You are to go back to your homes. There will be a period of transition in which the army will be guiding you. But democracy will return. Back to your homes. Go back home. Normality will be restored. The world is normal again.

(**JACK** *is whimpering on the floor.*)

What happened to this one?

SOLDIER 1. Feral. Mad. I can shoot him.

SOLDIER 2. No – leave him there. Alright – come along everybody – back to your homes.

(*The room is clearing –* **LISA** *comes forward from the crowd.*)

LISA. Jack it's me – Lisa. Do you know me – Lisa?

JACK. Mmmmgrrrmmrrr.

LISA. Lisa.

JACK. I. Me. Duh. Duh. Mad. Mad.

LISA. You're not mad Jack. Look at all the people. Babies.

JACK. Uh grrrroooo ooo.

LISA. No I wanna human.

(**STACY** *comes forward. She is eight months pregnant.*)

STACY. You alright Jack?

JACK. Grrrrrrr. Grrrrrrrr.

STACY. Jack – what's happened to you?

JACK. Grrrrrrrrrrrrr.

STACY. You're frightening.

BARRY. Come on love. Keep away.

STACY. Oooo. Felt something. I reckon this baby might come early.

BARRY. Shall we pick names?

STACY. Tonight? *(to* **LISA***)* Good luck.

> *(***BARRY*** puts his arm around* **STACY** *and they exit. It's just* **JACK**, **LISA** *and the* **MOTHER** *with the empty pram.)*

LISA. Come on Jack. Human words.

MOTHER. I got no baby. Pram's empty.

LISA. What you gonna do?

MOTHER. Search. It hasn't vanished.

LISA. Could have.

MOTHER. No. I'm a Mother. I've gotta find her.

JACK. L – l – l – listen.

> *(***JACK*** stands upright, human.)*

JACK. Th – th – th – There's…yeah… There's a place where people go to. They vanish. The people who…yeah.

MOTHER. I'll go there and bring her back. I'll carry on.

> *(Exit* **MOTHER** *with empty pram. Just* **JACK** *and* **LISA**.*)*

LISA. We're all back… Are you human?

JACK. Human. Yeah.

LISA. Good. I'm hungry. Is there food?

JACK. Lees. Where did you go?

LISA. Nowhere. Emptiness. It's a blank.

JACK. Think. Underworld? Spaceship?

LISA. I can't…

JACK. Parallel…?

LISA. You can ask as many times as you like.

JACK. You gotta remember something.

LISA. I don't. When you vanish there's nothing.

JACK. Maybe you'll get flashes or dreams or…?

LISA. Jack. Empty.

JACK. It'll come back. One day you'll know what there is.

LISA. Maybe.

JACK. You'll tell me. It's important.

LISA. What did you do?

JACK. Eh?

LISA. Six months on the planet. What did you do?

JACK. I don't know…

LISA. You're the only human being who knows.

JACK. I – nothing.

LISA. Yeah?

JACK. Did what I could to survive. Went out hunting. Did what I could for Stace and the baby. There was a baby. Until now she's… She's regressed. Hasn't had… But there was a baby then. I kept things going. Fought. Protected.

LISA. Like an animal?

JACK. You have to.

LISA. They'll be rebuilding the world now.

JACK. No more rhinoceros up the shopping centre.

LISA. So you can be a human being yeah?

JACK. Do my best. Do you think it was aliens?

LISA. Stop.

JACK. Maybe if you tried drawing or…

LISA. Just stop.

JACK. Hypnosis to –

LISA. Stop. Stop. Stop. Listen. You are never going to know. Face it. It's not going to –

JACK. The mother of my – everyone's been there. Secret. And I don't know it. It's impossible. Can't live with that.

LISA. There's no choice.

JACK. I want to see inside their heads, their memories –

LISA. No.

JACK. Cut 'em open: where did you go? Where did you go? Where did you go?

LISA. Stop it Jack – you're horrible.

JACK. How am I supposed to spend the rest of my life with you if you got a secret?

LISA. It's not a –

JACK. I can't do that.

LISA. If you want you can go. Leave. There's the door.

JACK. Yeah.

LISA. You can pack and leave if that's how you feel.

JACK. Maybe.

LISA. Run off.

JACK. Yeah.

LISA. Go on.

JACK. Yeah. That's best. If I never know you…

>*(long pause)*

LISA. You're still here.

JACK. I know.

>*(long pause)*

I know.

>*(long pause)*

Yeah.

>*(Long pause. He touches her stomach.)*

Yeah.